KU-260-362

178

This Ladybird Book belongs to:

_____

_____

_____

_____

This Ladybird retelling
by
Raymond Sibley

Published by Ladybird Books Ltd
80 Strand London WC2R 0RL
A Penguin Company
7 9 10 8
© LADYBIRD BOOKS LTD 1993

Printed in Italy

FAVOURITE TALES

Snow White
and the Seven Dwarfs

illustrated
by
MARTIN AITCHISON

based on the story by Jacob and Wilhelm Grimm

Every day the Queen would stand in front of her mirror and ask,

*"Mirror, mirror, on the wall,
Who is the fairest of us all?"*

And the mirror would reply,

"Thou, O Queen, art the fairest of all!"

But Snow White was growing up and becoming more lovely every day.

One day, when the Queen asked,

"Mirror, mirror, on the wall,
Who is the fairest of us all?"

the mirror gave a new reply.

"O Queen, Snow White is fairest of all!"

The Queen grew pale with rage.

From that day on, the Queen hated
Snow White with all her heart. Every
day the girl grew more and more
beautiful. In her fury, the Queen sent
for a huntsman.

"Take Snow White into the forest,"
she ordered. "Kill her and bring her
heart back to me."

So the huntsman took Snow White
into the forest, but he could not kill
the lovely girl. "Run," he said gruffly,
"and never return!"

Snow White was lost and frightened.
"Oh where shall I go?" she wept. At
last she glimpsed a little cottage in a
clearing.

Cold and tired, Snow White peeped inside. What an odd little place it was! There were seven tiny chairs and seven tiny plates. Along one wall, there were seven little beds.

As there was no one about, Snow White lay down on one of the beds and fell fast asleep.

Unknown to the sleeping girl, the cottage belonged to seven dwarfs, who worked in the mines all day. At nightfall, they came home from their work and lit seven candles.

"Goodness me, there's someone here!" cried one of the dwarfs in surprise, when he saw Snow White.

The noise woke Snow White, and the seven little dwarfs crowded round her. "How beautiful she is!" they cried.

"Why have you come here, my dear, and how can we help you?" asked one of the dwarfs in a gentle voice.

Snow White explained about the wicked Queen. As she told her story, she grew so sad that she began to cry.

"Hush, my dear," said the kind little men. "You can live here with us, safe from that evil woman." Snow White gratefully accepted their offer.

In the palace, the Queen once again stood before her magic mirror. She did not know that the huntsman had disobeyed her and brought her an animal's heart instead of Snow White's.

Rubbing her hands with glee, the Queen smiled and said,

"Mirror, mirror, on the wall,
Who is the fairest of us all?"

And the mirror replied,

"O Queen, Snow White is fairest of all.
For in the forest,
where seven dwarfs dwell,
Snow White is still
alive and well."

Screaming with rage, the Queen planned her revenge.

Next morning, after the dwarfs left for work, Snow White sang happily to herself as she tidied the little house.

Before long an old pedlar woman knocked at the door. It was the Queen in disguise. "Come and look at these pretty things, dear child," she cackled.

Snow White was enchanted.

She let the old woman tie a pink velvet ribbon around her neck to see how it would look. Suddenly, the old woman pulled the ribbon tight! Snow White fell to the ground.

The dwarfs found Snow White lying close to death. They untied the ribbon so she could breathe, and by the next morning she was well again.

"That pedlar was the wicked Queen!" said the dwarfs. Before they left for work, they made Snow White promise never to open the door to anyone.

Meanwhile, once again, the magic mirror had told the wicked Queen that Snow White was not dead.

The angry Queen disguised herself as a kind old lady selling combs. Again, Snow White nearly died, for the combs were poisoned.

This time the dwarfs were very cross. "Do not let *anyone* into the house," they said firmly.

When the mirror told the Queen that she had failed again, she was furious. She was determined that Snow White should die.

Next day the Queen took a basket of poisoned apples and tapped on the cottage window.

"I don't need to come in," she said cunningly, "but do try this lovely apple, dear child. It's delicious!"

Snow White could see no harm in a shiny red apple, so she took a big bite.

When the dwarfs came home, they found Snow White lifeless on the floor. They did everything they could to save her, but it was no use. She lay cold and still.

"We have lost the loveliest girl that ever lived," they sobbed.

Far away in the palace, the Queen stood proudly before her mirror.

"Mirror, mirror, on the wall,
Who is the fairest of us all?"

And the mirror answered at last,

"Thou, O Queen, art the fairest of all."

As the Prince's servants were carrying the coffin down the mountain, they stumbled. Suddenly a piece of apple, which had been caught in Snow White's throat, fell out!

Snow White opened her eyes and saw the handsome Prince. "I love you," he whispered. "Please say that you will marry me." Snow White smiled happily.

The dwarfs, overjoyed that their
beloved Snow White was alive, waved
goodbye as she rode off with the
Prince.

Soon Snow White and her prince
were married. They lived happily ever
after – and the wicked Queen and her
mirror were never heard of again!